BEST PLAY

A PERFECT PLAY NOVELLA

LAYLA REYNE

Best Play

Copyright © 2024 by Layla Reyne

All rights reserved. No part of this book may be reproduced or transmitted in any form or by any means, electronic or mechanical, including photocopying, recording, or by any information storage and retrieval system without the written permission of the copyright owner, and where permitted by law. Reviewers may quote brief passages in a review.

Cover Design: Cate Ashwood Designs

Cover Photography: Wander Aguiar Photography

Editing: Adam Mongaya

Proofreading: Lori Parks

First Edition

June, 2024

E-Book ISBN: 978-1-962010-18-4

Paperback ISBN: 978-1-962010-19-1

This is a work of fiction. Names, characters, places, and incidents are either the product of the author's imagination or are used fictitiously. Any resemblance to actual persons living or dead, business establishments, events, or locales is entirely coincidental. All person(s) depicted on the cover are model(s) used for illustrative purposes only. The author acknowledges the copyrights and trademarked status and trademark owners of any trademarks and copyrights mentioned in this work of fiction.

Content Warnings: Explicit sex; explicit language; off-page death of a former spouse; mentions of PTSD, anxiety, depression, and past suicide attempt of an off-page character.

ABOUT THIS BOOK

When the best play is the marriage already made...

By Friday, Agents Bishop and Marshall must:
Solve an anything-but-routine burglary.
Determine why the house's previous owner was murdered.
Avoid getting killed in the process.

Because on Saturday, Levi and Marsh must:
Keep an overdue promise to their son.
Entertain a house full of friends and family.
Say "I do" in the wedding their marriage of convenience
turned true love deserves.

Marsh and Levi are determined to help a friend in need.
But they're already six months late for a very important
date.
If they're not at the altar on time for their Christmas (in
July) wedding, they'll face their most terrifying enemy yet
—their teenage son.

Best Play is the fourth book in the M/M romantic suspense series, Perfect Play. This series epilogue novella features Marsh and Levi at their steamy partnership best, as they make their way to the altar a second, forever time.

For David

ONE

"HOW DID I end up in *this* outfit?" Levi tied the pink bandana around his neck, tucked the loose ends beneath the collar of his fringed, black-and-white, Western-style shirt, then stepped back, giving himself a once-over in the guest bedroom mirror. He plucked the white Stetson Marsh had gifted him off the bed and flipped it onto his head. Outfit complete, but still . . . "I could've rocked the pink."

"I'm sure you could," came Marsh's voice from behind him. "But I rock it better."

Glancing up, Levi caught the reflection of his husband in the mirror and—*Oh.*

Better was an understatement, and fuck if Levi could decide where to look, his attention torn in a dozen different directions. From Marsh's bronze skin and sprinkling of chest hair on full display between the open flaps of the hot pink vest. To his muscled biceps and rippling abs as he sauntered closer. To the hot pink bell bottoms Marsh had somehow poured himself into, his thighs testing the seams, his shiny belt buckle drawing Levi's gaze to his cock that was likewise testing his zipper.

"Jesus fuck," Levi cursed.

"Haven't we been over this?" Marsh snaked his arms around Levi's waist and pressed close behind him. Heat, so much heat, up and down the length of Levi's body, then in his ear, as Marsh whispered hotly, "Not Jesus, just Marsh." He nipped his neck above the bandana, then lifted his hands and began unsnapping Levi's shiny shirt buttons. "And you're wearing entirely too much clothing."

He got as far as Levi's ribs, the brush of Marsh's warm, rough fingertips against his skin sending another wave of heat crashing through him, finally knocking Levi out of his pink-on-bronze haze. "And you're not wearing nearly enough." He turned in Marsh's arms and grabbed the lapels of his vest. "I can't believe your mom made this for you." He tried and failed to tug the vest closed. "Will this thing even button?"

Marsh stole the hat from his head, tossed it onto the dresser beside his matching one, then stepped into Levi's space, forcing him back a step. Then another, and another, until Levi bumped into the bedroom door. Dipping his head, Marsh peppered his exposed collarbone with kisses. "I think you're missing the point of San Francisco Pride." Then altered his path and continued the kisses up the column of his throat to the corner of Levi's mouth. "And of a bachelor party."

He splayed his big, warm hands over Levi's chest, branding as he pushed the shirt open wider, and fuck it, how was Levi supposed to resist? He angled his face and brought their lips crashing together, greedily sucking

Marsh's tongue as it swept inside his mouth. The fire that burned between them was no less scorching now than it had been that night a year ago after his cousin's wedding, when Marsh had held him in his arms and given him exactly what he'd needed. What he'd asked for that night, during the whirlwind month that had followed, and over the past year, which had been one of the best of his life. A life—another shot at love—that Levi had thought out of his reach until a cocky cowboy had reached out to him.

He smiled against Marsh's lips. "I love you."

Marsh shoved a knee between his thighs and rocked their hips together. "You love my cock."

"That too," Levi said before a flash of light in the mirror drew his gaze, the midday sun catching his wedding ring on the hand clutching his husband's ass. A perfect one at that, encased in hot pink. Levi flexed his fingers, more of that light shining, more of Marsh rubbing up against him. "Maybe we skip the bachelor party." Marsh chuckled against him, his big body rippling in Levi's arms. "I don't see a bachelor in this room. Hell, I think the only one in this house is David."

Marsh drew back and braced a forearm beside Levi's head, his dark eyes sparkling with heat and affection, with all the love Levi felt in his own chest. "Yes, our son," Marsh said, "who we owe this party, like we owe him a wedding next weekend." He lifted his knee, pressing it snug against the underside of Levi's balls, making Levi gasp. Marsh's smirk was the same devastating one that had hooked him from across a dinner table a year ago. "And we owe ourselves a first anniversary celebration."

"Best deal I ever made."

Marsh's grin gentled as he pressed his lips to Levi's. "Thank you."

"For?"

"Saying yes. That night and all the days and nights since."

"Fuck." Levi clutched his sides, hauling him closer. "Just when I think I can't love you more." He flipped them, backing Marsh against the door and diving in for more of his husband's kisses. He spread a hand over Marsh's chest, over the beating heart of the man he'd promised to love and cherish a year ago, words of convenience then. He couldn't wait to repeat them, full of conviction now, but first . . .

He slid his hand down, cupping Marsh's erection and stroking. "How about a private celebration before the festivities begin?"

Marsh thrust into his grip. "I can agree to that deal."

Their son, however, did not. "Dad! Marsh!" He shouted from the other side of the door, fists banging the wood, rattling them against it. "You're supposed to be putting on clothes, not taking them off."

Levi buried his face in Marsh's chest, burying his laughter. David knew them too well. Knew to recruit help too.

"Texas!" Lily screamed at the top of her lungs as she smacked the door in that open-palmed way Levi remembered from David's toddler days a decade ago. "Hurry up!"

"No tag teaming," Marsh called back through his own laughter.

"I needed help," David argued. "And Reese isn't here yet."

They'd been to San Francisco so often the past year, either for work or for visiting friends and family, like Lily and her dads, that David had gone and gotten himself a Bay Area boyfriend. Hadn't lost the teenager attitude, though. "You two are impossible," he grumbled.

"We'll be down in five," Levi called back to him.

"How many seconds is that?" Lily asked, still at the top of her lungs.

"Three hundred," David answered.

"I can't count that high yet."

"Good thing I have a stopwatch on my phone," he said, ever patient with her, if not with them. A few seconds of indecipherable whispering later, Lily gave them a stern "Clock's ticking!" warning before the two troublemakers trudged off, cackling.

"So much for that private celebration," Levi grumbled, taking after his son.

"Tonight, baby." Marsh nipped his bottom lip and tugged at the bandana around his neck. "I promise to put this to good use."

Levi groaned. "Not helping at all." As much as he wanted to sink into Marsh again, to drop to his knees and take care of the erection still persistently pressed against his thigh, he reluctantly pushed back and straightened his clothes. "And you better keep that promise."

"I intend to." Marsh tossed him his Stetson before flipping his own onto his head, then opening the door. "After you."

At the top of the stairs, Levi paused to let the familiar sounds from below—of a family celebrating together—wash over him.

Marsh stepped to his side, a hand on his opposite hip. "Everything okay?"

Levi tipped back his head so he could catch his husband's gaze from under the brims of their hats. "Thank you for this too. For giving me and David more laughter, more love, more family."

Carefully avoiding a collision, Marsh leaned in and pecked his lips. "Yours is pretty great too."

"And they'll *all* be together next weekend."

Marsh shivered. "Little terrifying."

"Lotta terrifying," Levi said, even as a grin stretched across his face. As he pressed that smile to his husband's. "But I wouldn't have it any other way when I say 'I do' to you again."

TWO

MARSH LOUNGED at the large round table in the center of Under the Table's dining room, sipping a bottle of Gravity Stout and glancing around the restaurant full of friends and family. Jax's girlfriend, February, owned the place, and she had closed it for Marsh and Levi's post-Pride parade bachelor party. At the table on one side of Marsh was his best friend and best man, Brax, who was pretending to pay attention to the hacker speak between his husband, Holt, Agent Farmer, who'd flown up from San Diego, and Jamie Walker, a family friend who used to be an FBI cyber agent and now coached basketball at one of the local Division I colleges.

On Marsh's other side, a leering Agent Cameron Byrne had his dark eyes trained on the heavily tattooed silver fox behind the bar. Dressed in a pink fringe vest, frayed jeans, and rainbow glitter cuffs that matched his rainbow glitter combat boots, Cam's husband, San Francisco's US Attorney, was popping caps off bottles of beer while Jax and Levi slung cocktails.

"If I hadn't seen him at work," Marsh said to Cam, "I'd think your husband was more at home behind a bar than in a courtroom."

"Might still be true," Cam said with a grin. "Same as your husband."

Marsh held his beer bottle out for a clink, Cam tapping back with the neck of his. "Touché." Levi had waited tables all through college and usually played host for his family's get-togethers in San Diego. As for Dominic Price, not only was he a federal prosecutor, but he also co-owned one of the most popular microbreweries in the Bay Area.

"Last call on the Imperial Stout!" Nic shouted to the crowd, and Cam bolted out of his seat. "That fucker was holding out on me."

Chuckling, Marsh settled back in his and glanced around again at the charming space, wishing for a place like it in San Diego. A bright, white shiplap roof arched overhead, jewel tone booths and chairs invited guests to get comfy, and a kick-ass bar provided plenty of live-action entertainment. He wasn't surprised folks gravitated around it. "This place is pretty fantastic."

Brax glanced around, same as he'd done, but with a certain fondness in his hazel eyes. "Would you believe it was riddled with bullet holes four months ago?"

"Absolutely," Marsh said with a knowing grin.

Feb had wandered her way into the Madigans' world—or, more accurately, the Madigans had wandered their way into hers—so yeah, no surprise chaos had erupted. But so too had love for Holt and Brax's hacker-hunter protégé, Jax.

"But you missed one in the bar." Marsh pointed at the

round hole on the opposite side of the bar from where Levi was mixing what looked like a Negroni.

"Intentional," Brax said. "Feb thought it gave the place more character."

Marsh laughed out loud. "No wonder she fits in so well."

"Hate to interrupt, fellas," Helena said from over Brax's shoulder. "But Lily is standing guard by the pantry door. She says David needs protection from, and I quote, 'that asshole.'"

Marsh's gut sank, figuring he knew what this was about, at the same time he bit back a laugh imagining Brax's daughter, tiny fists on her hips, uttering those words. She was as fiery as her red hair—and as quick to pick up words and skills as the rest of her family.

On the other side of Brax, Holt broke midsentence and jerked around in his chair, glaring up at his sister. "And where did she learn that word?"

"No idea," Auntie Helena said with a flit of her fingers before she danced away.

Brax hung his head, shaking it in defeat. "We're so doomed."

Marsh patted his best man's back. "If you didn't know that already where Lily was concerned . . ."

"Oh, we know," Holt said, moving to stand.

"Stay," Marsh said, already on his feet. "I'll send her your way." He caught Levi's gaze as he wove through the tables, tipping his head toward the kitchen breezeway.

Levi met him there. "What's going on?"

Marsh hated to deepen the divot that had already formed between his brows. Today was supposed to be filled with fun and smiles, but teenage hearts didn't care for adults' timelines. "Boy troubles, I'm afraid."

Lips pressed together, he took only a second to reach the same conclusion Marsh had. "I haven't seen Reese since we first got here."

"Me either." Hand in the small of his husband's back, Marsh led him down the breezeway and around the outside edge of the kitchen where February, Hawes, and Celia were prepping dessert trays with Celia's daughter, Mia.

"Texas!" came a loud, high-pitched shout as soon as they rounded the last corner. In front of the pantry door, Lily looked exactly as Marsh had imagined, red ringlets wild, color high on her freckled cheeks, tiny hands fisted on her hips. "Reese was an as—"

"Language!" David shouted from the other side of the door, and even through wood and over the kitchen noise, Marsh could hear the tears in his voice.

"He left," Lily declared, standing firm.

"I told him to," David countered.

Marsh crouched in front of Lily and gently palmed her shoulder. One protector to another. "You did good, sweetheart. Thank you," he told the tiny, scary tyke. Definitely a Madigan. "We can take it from here."

She didn't look convinced. Thankfully, Mia knew the way to her cousin's heart. "Hey, Lily, you want to help me with these cupcakes?"

She bit her lip, big brown eyes darting between them and Mia. "You got this?"

"We got it," Levi assured her.

She didn't need to be told twice, the siren call of frosting too tempting to resist. Marsh accepted Levi's hand up and mouthed a *Thank you* to Mia.

"Can you toss me the candied ginger from in there?" she called.

Marsh nodded while Levi knocked on the door. "David, can we come in?"

The bottle of ginger appeared first, then a tear-stained David. His cheeks were as red as Lily's had been, albeit for a different reason, and Marsh's heart broke for the kid. He tossed the bottle to Mia, then slid inside the pantry, leaving the door cracked this time in case anyone needed them for something else. He leaned back against the shelves while Levi sat cross-legged on the floor next to David.

"What happened?" Levi asked.

"Reese is a freshman next year, and he—" His words caught on a tearful hiccup, and Levi slung an arm around his shoulders, hugging him tight against his side. "He didn't even want to spend the rest of the summer together."

Marsh and Levi had worried this was coming. Reese was two years older than David, and while the rising freshman had clearly been into David when they'd spent time together in San Francisco, he hadn't made much time for David otherwise. David, despite his and Levi's warnings, had gotten attached, though Marsh suspected it was more to the idea of a boyfriend than to Reese himself, given the two didn't have much in common.

He pushed off the shelves and crouched in front of David, hand on his son's knee. "Reese doesn't know what he's missing."

David glanced up, then away, his free arm flopping at his side. "I mean, I knew it wasn't long-term." Sniffling, he reached behind Levi and grabbed a napkin from the stack on the shelf he'd clearly already raided, judging by the mountain of tissue balls at his feet. "It wouldn't last with him at Duke and me at Davis, assuming I get in there. But I thought maybe I'd get a trip to North Carolina out of it."

"We don't need Reese for that," Marsh said. His other best friend, Sean, owned a house with his wife and husband right on the Carolina coast. "We can go to Casa Henby-Paxton whenever you want."

David returned his gaze to them, eyes bright. "For real?"

Snickering, Levi rose and lightly kicked Marsh's knee. "You so got played."

Marsh shook his head. "Nope, I got a trip to Hanover out of it." He reached out a hand to David, palm out for a high five. "Wins all around. We can check calendars for some dates after the wedding."

David's momentary uplift faded. "I don't have a date to the wedding now."

"Which makes *you*"—Marsh pointed at him—"the most eligible bachelor."

"And you're my best man," Levi said. "You and Brax are gonna have your hands full."

"Yes, we know how well you two get where you're supposed to be on time." His heavy sigh was half annoyed teen and half beleaguered Uncle Brax. If Marsh didn't know better, he would've bet Brax had been in his son's life for longer than just a year.

"Well, then, you two," Marsh said, offering him a hand up, "better get your plan in place." He drew David into a hug, embracing him as tightly as Levi had. "Seriously, kid, Reese doesn't know what he's missing."

"You're right," David said. "He doesn't." With a final honking blow of his nose, he gathered up his tissues and pushed out of the pantry, some of his confidence restored and a mission to distract him. He tossed the tissues in the trash, washed his hands, and called to his partner in crime. "Lily! Triple team time!"

Levi waited until they'd disappeared up the breezeway to release the sigh Marsh figured he'd been holding in since they'd first stepped into the pantry. "His first breakup in the books," Levi said, sounding a little sad but also more than a little relieved.

Marsh held the pantry door open for them, then slung an arm around his waist as they made their way out of the kitchen. "You never liked that guy anyway." Truth be told, Marsh wasn't sure anyone would ever be good enough for their son in either of their eyes.

He didn't have a chance to contemplate that further, though. Jamie and his husband, Special Agent in Charge Aidan Talley, met them halfway down the breezeway with their FBI faces on, even though Jamie was years out of the Bureau at this point.

"What's going on?" Levi asked, straightening from Marsh's side, the both of them clicking into LEO mode as quickly as their friends had similarly shifted.

"Break-in at one of my former player's homes," Jamie said. "In San Diego."

THREE

"AND THIS," Jamie said, after introducing Brax and Marsh, "is Assistant Special Agent in Charge, Levi Bishop."

Levi wrangled his gaze from the ocean view out the balcony doors and extended his attention and hand to the young man standing with them in the middle of his Cardiff home's living area. "It's nice to meet you, Press."

Presley Jackson played basketball for one of the teams in LA, but years before going pro, he'd played at Charlotte University when Jamie had been undercover as a coach there. After impressing at CU, Press had transferred to a D-I school and led his team to a national championship.

"Nice to meet you too." Press returned the shake, then glanced around again at their gathered group, including Aidan. "Though, no offense, this seems like a lot of folks for a break-in."

Levi jutted a thumb at Marsh. "We're getting married this weekend. Again."

Marsh, in turn, jutted his thumb at Brax. "And he's my best man, so he was already along for the ride."

"Well, I appreciate it," Press said with a chuckle. "It's certainly more interest than the one local cop on Saturday night showed." Jamie had told them about how the brush-off by the San Diego County sheriff's department, which served as local law enforcement for Cardiff, was a big reason why Press had reached out to him yesterday. That and he'd been pretty rattled.

"We'll get to that," Levi said as their group carefully followed Press through the tossed living area to the balcony where the furniture was still intact. "But why don't you start by telling us what happened."

"Yeah, so, you know I play in LA. Got a condo up there near the facility. But season's over. Been over for us for a while." He rolled his eyes and swiped a hand over his shaved head. "Anyway, I wanted to spend some time here since I just bought the place and I'm part-time at UCSD."

"Press is getting his law degree," Jamie said, pride brimming over in his voice as he patted Press's back.

A blush reddened Press's dark cheeks. "Promised my mom and best friend."

"How long ago did you buy the place?" Aidan asked.

"Closed the Friday before Memorial Day."

"And everything was okay at first?" Brax said.

"Yeah, first couple weeks were great." He stretched an arm out toward the glass and metal balcony wall. "I mean, look at that view."

"It's stunning," Levi concurred. West of the 5 and situated on a bluff over the San Elijo Lagoon, Press's place had a view that extended all the way to the Pacific Ocean. It was a hell of a perch; the sunsets would be amazing.

"Would sell anyone," Marsh replied. "But it's also isolated up here."

"Also what sold me on it, until the break-in." Press folded his arms, fingers digging into his biceps. "I got home late Saturday. Been studying with classmates for an exam later this week. I was so tired I didn't even realize the house alarm was off. Took the elevator up from the garage, flicked on the lights, and found the place trashed. Ripped sectional cushions on the floor, cabinets and drawers open, pictures down off the walls. Then there was a crash from out here. The balcony doors were open, so I guess whoever it was ran out this way."

Levi peered over to the balcony wall. "That's a steep drop."

"No shit," Press said. "And I sure as hell wasn't chasing him over it."

"Him?"

"Yeah, bulky dude. White from what I could see of his neck between the mask and jacket he wore. Also saw a car waiting for him at the bottom."

"Make and model?" Marsh asked as he stepped beside Levi.

"Old four-door of some sort. Sorry, it was dark out and so was the car."

Marsh craned over the balcony, glancing left and right, then pointed at the intersection and signal lights to the north. "I'll pull cams." He rotated back around, leaning against the rail. "About what time was this?"

"Just before ten," Press answered. "I was about to call —" His abrupt halt drew Levi back around and Brax and

Aidan to the edge of their seats, the SAC beating Levi to his next question.

"Why did you buy this place?" Aidan said. "You could've gotten into a law school in LA. Somewhere closer to the facility and your place up there."

The baller blushed again, deeper this time. "Well, I won't be playing forever, and I don't love LA."

"But you do love someone here," Levi surmised, following the clues in Press's carefully chosen words and his less carefully hidden reactions.

His gaze flickered to Levi and Marsh, then bounced to Jamie, a safer, more familiar ear for him. "He's got a job here, a good one, so I figured I'd put down some roots too, for whenever I decide to stop playing."

Jamie clasped his shoulder. "He's a lucky guy."

"I'm the lucky one," Press said, the corners of his lips turned up in a shy smile, clearly smitten. Maybe even in love. But if so, why hadn't he mentioned the boyfriend to Jamie? Where was he now?

"Have you been staying with him since the break-in?" Levi asked. It had been two nights now—the night of the incident, then last night, when, after no follow-up from the sheriff's department, Press had called Jamie. "Doesn't look like you've been here much."

"No, he's . . . umm . . . out of town. Special occasion. I didn't want to bother him." Chin ducked, he ran his hand over his head again. "I've been at a hotel near campus."

While Levi was curious what Press was holding back, he sensed Press would be more comfortable having that conversation with Jamie. And Levi didn't sense it was relevant to the case; Press didn't seem the sort who would hold back that kind of information, especially not after calling them in to help. Levi circled back to an earlier, more relevant thread instead. "What did the local officer say? The one who was here Saturday night."

"Random break-in."

"Was anything missing?" Aidan asked.

Press shook his head. "Nothing as far as I can tell. Just trashed the place, then ran." He gestured again at the balcony wall. "I mean, what could he carry out and over?"

"Your championship ring," Jamie said.

"Nope," Press said. "Still in the glass case on my desk."

"Anything else small and valuable like that?" Brax asked. "A safe with cash or papers?"

Press shook his head. "Nope and nope. Nothing's missing as far as I can tell."

"What do you know about the house?" Marsh asked.

"That I got it for *way* cheaper than everything else around here. Figured it was the highway noise." As if on cue, a car horn blew from not far off, some Monday morning commuter clearly unhappy about the traffic. Press, however, didn't seem too bothered by it. "I can close the balcony doors and hardly hear it."

"We'll look into it," Jamie said before his gaze strayed to Marsh's, and Levi could practically hear their hacker game plan coming together.

"Could it have been someone targeting you?" Brax gently asked. "You are kind of famous."

"Not *that* famous. Definitely not his kind of famous," he said with a head tilt toward Jamie. "So that leaves who? The asshole I beat at mock trial?" He shrugged again. "Whoever it was, he ran away when I got here."

"I'd still like to put a protection detail on you, especially if you intend to stay here," Levi said.

"I'll stay at my boyfriend's place. He's back today and also former military, so I'm all set for protection."

"You sure?"

"We're good."

"All righty, then," Levi said, letting the matter of protection and Press's boyfriend go again for now, intending to have Jamie follow up in a less my-living-room-is-full-of-LEOs manner. "Let us do some digging and see what we can find out."

"Do you have the contact info for the local officer who responded Saturday night?" Marsh asked.

"Detective Hines." Press fished his wallet from his back pocket, withdrew a card, and handed it to Marsh, who snapped a picture with his phone before passing it back. "We'll reach out, then be in touch."

"I'll check in too," Jamie said. "And keep me posted if you run into any more trouble."

"Yeah, Coach," Press said with a nod. "Thanks for calling in the cavalry."

"Least I could do," Jamie replied, drawing his former player into another hug, then walking and talking next season with him and Aidan as they all made their way downstairs to the garage.

Levi hung back with Marsh and Brax, the latter of whom asked, "Chance it's a random B&E?"

"If this were Oceanside or downtown San Diego," Levi said, "fifty-fifty."

Marsh finished his thought. "But here in Cardiff, single digits."

FOUR

"AND HOW IS this case in our jurisdiction?" SAC Kwan asked from her seat at the head of the conference table. She'd missed the festivities in San Francisco, holding down the fort here in SD while her ASAC was gone.

"It's not," Marsh admitted. With two SACs in the room, no use beating around the bush. "But the sheriff's department isn't paying attention."

"Which is why we're going to tread carefully," Levi said. "Try not to draw it."

"Neither of you are even supposed to be here," Kwan said, sounding five-o'clock exasperated with them when it was barely noon. "You're supposed to be off this week getting ready for your re-wedding."

Marsh smirked at his old Army buddy turned boss. "Aww, come on, Eagle, you know me better than that."

"And we all know your husband is a workaholic," Farmer said as he cruised into the conference room, suitcase rolling at his side.

"Hey, now," Levi feigned offense. "You're the one who came straight here from the airport."

"Hey, now," the cyber agent parroted back with a grin as he flopped into the open seat beside Aidan. "Maybe if someone"—he jostled the Irishman's side—"had a bigger private jet."

Laughter echoed around the table until Levi cleared his throat, drawing them all to relative order again. "As I was saying, we tread carefully."

"We can still put protection on Press," Brax said. "I know he said he didn't need any, but I also didn't like what I saw at the house."

"Me neither," Aidan agreed. "That burglar was hunting for something when Press interrupted him. He'll be back."

"Wait, what?" All humor gone, Farmer lurched to the edge of his seat, his entire frame vibrating with military-ready energy, how Marsh imagined the former paratrooper must have felt standing at the aircraft door before each jump. "Are you talking about Presley Jackson? The professional basketball player? That's why y'all left so early this morning?"

Marsh nodded. "Break-in at his place in Cardiff on Saturday night. He called Jamie yesterday after the local cops blew him off."

"He played for me at Charlotte University," Jamie explained. "As coaches, we're not supposed to have favorites, but we all do. Press is one of mine. I want to help him out and help keep him safe."

"Press says he's covered. His boyfriend's former military," Levi told Kwan, then cut a glance at Marsh, Farmer, and Brax, all of them vets too. "But I agree with the team. I'd like to get additional protection on him."

"I've got him," Farmer volunteered.

"We need you hacking," Marsh countered. Farmer was the second-best cyber agent in the San Diego field office, behind him, and he had a knack for finding the needle in a haystack. "You, Jamie, and I are gonna dig through all the real estate records for the house Press bought. See who else might have an interest in it. And if that search turns up nothing, we dig into Press."

To his credit, Jamie didn't object, the former agent understanding and accepting the investigative protocol. "I'm in."

"Me too," Farmer said. "*And* I can do protection detail." When he still didn't get the approval he needed from Kwan and Levi, he pitched harder. "Look, not gonna lie, I'm a fan, but more importantly, if his boyfriend is former military, he may take more kindly to another vet on guard duty versus someone he considers less qualified." When all the nonvets around the table opened their mouths to object, Farmer beat them to it. "*Wrong,* of course, but ask Marsh or Brax or the SAC how military folk think."

"He's not wrong," Kwan said, then to Levi, "Write up the detail with Farmer."

Levi nodded, then turned his attention to Aidan. "Which leaves us going back to the house with a crime scene unit, if you're game?"

Aidan nodded. "Top to bottom since it sounds like local only eyeballed it."

"I can help too," Brax said. "Talk to some neighbors while you're inside."

"Nuh-uh-uh," Marsh said. "I've got a special job for my best man."

Brax hung back his head on a heavy sigh, as beleaguered as ever. "Do I even want to know?"

Marsh slung an arm over his friend's shoulders, grinning. "Moms are due at the airport in an hour. I'm sure Irina can't wait to ogle the best man's ass."

The room erupted with laughter again, including Levi, and after a very early, very long morning, Marsh counted it a win.

FIVE

THE DASHBOARD CLOCK read midnight as Levi pulled the RX into the garage at home. A too-long workday on what was supposed to be a no-work day, but he was happy to do this favor for Jamie, and he was heartened by how his team had stepped up to help too. Including the snoring man beside him. He gave him a gentle shake. "We're home, babe."

Marsh lolled his head on the headrest, face tilted toward Levi. "Can I just sleep here?" he grumbled, eyes still closed.

Chuckling, Levi leaned across the console and pecked his lips, then, using the distraction and opportunity, unfastened Marsh's seat belt and opened his door. "Let's go, cowboy. I promise the bed is comfier."

Marsh grumbled some more, but, as Levi had learned about his husband, the siren call of the bed at the end of a long day was irresistible. He followed the lead Levi had left for him, climbing out of the car, grabbing his hat from the back, and meeting Levi at the interior door to the house. Before he got it open, though, the door to David's room off the back of the garage swung open. Their son looked ready for bed, dressed in a stolen FBI gym tee and wrinkled sleep pants, but the headphones around his neck and the game controller in his hand indicated otherwise.

"It's past time for you to go to sleep," Levi said.

"I'm off this week," David said with an insolent teen shrug. Definitely back to himself. "You two were supposed to be off too."

"Why?" Marsh said. He pushed off the doorjamb, tossed his hat to Levi, and crossed to David, looping an arm around his neck and dragging him into a sideways hug. "We've got the best wedding planner in San Diego."

David twisted out of his hold and split a glare between them. "Whatever you're doing, be done with it by Friday."

"Roger that." Marsh gave him a salute, then, grabbing his hat back from Levi, flipped it onto his head and disappeared into the house.

For his part, Levi gave his son a less rambunctious version of the hug he'd endured from Marsh. "You good?" he asked.

"Yeah, fine." David, thankfully, hadn't withdrawn into himself like he would have done before Marsh had come into their lives, before the cowboy had brought them each back to a place where they could communicate and heal after losing David's mom. To where they could be a family again. "It was a madhouse here tonight with the grandmas, but Nona and Pop came over, and Brax and I cooked." An even larger family than either of them could have imagined, Marsh coming with two moms and the Madigans and, by extension, the Talleys and their crew. "There's leftovers in the fridge."

"But what about *you*?" Levi asked again. "How are you? Anything from Reese?"

"Fuck him."

"Lang—"

David raised a hand, and his green eyes were as fiery as late mother's. "If there's a time I'm allowed to curse, this is it."

He had a point. "Fair," Levi agreed. "Fuck him. But, truth, how are you?"

"Good." He rotated back into his room, tossed his game controller in his desk chair, then folded onto the futon, one leg under him, the other hiked, chin resting on his knee. "It's good having all the family around, even if it is Grand Central here."

Levi leaned a shoulder against the jamb. "Anywhere you need me and Marsh tomorrow?"

"Not tomorrow," he said, raking a hand through his ginger curls, a frizzy halo this time of night. "I need you both Wednesday night for the cookout. Trevor will be here, and I cannot guarantee I won't lose my shit."

Levi stifled his laugh, barely, David's crush on Charlie and Sean's husband no less diminished. "Maybe we'll have this case done by then."

David snickered. "Someone's optimistic for midnight." Eyes rolling, he slumped back in the futon. "Just be done by Friday."

"Anyone ever tell you you're an awesome kid and wedding planner?"

"Remember that when you get your credit card bill for this week."

"Also fair," Levi said with a laugh. "Now, I'm going to

bed before we do all the chaos again tomorrow." He turned for the house door, but David's softer, more serious "Hey, Dad?" had him turning back around.

"Danger level?" David asked.

It was a system they'd developed after last summer, a way for Levi and Marsh to be as honest as they could be with David about the danger involved with their work, with whatever particular case or cases they were working. And if last summer had been a ten out of ten, then this case . . . "Three out of ten."

"Good," David said. "Get done by Friday."

"Roger that," Levi said, echoing Marsh's sign-off, before he headed inside himself.

He found Marsh at the kitchen island plating leftovers. "Eat," he said, pushing a plate of grilled chicken kebab and couscous in front of the closest barstool. "We forgot to today."

Levi claimed the seat, then waited for Marsh to take the one beside him. "We're off the wedding hook until Wednesday night," he told Marsh as he pried a morsel of chicken and a charred pepper off the skewer. He popped it into his mouth and hummed appreciatively at the flavorful bite. "We need to bang this out tomorrow if we can. For our sakes and for Press's. He's got enough stress as it is, by the sound of it."

"He's impressive. Basketball career and law school." Marsh dredged a piece of chicken through the red pepper spread he'd heaped on his plate. "We'll go through everything with fresh eyes in the morning."

They finished their food, Marsh clearing the plates and . . .

A gentle shake brought Levi back to where he'd fallen asleep cheek down on the bar. "Let's go, Wolfy," Marsh said, using the nickname that always made Levi smile, had him burrowing into Marsh's side as they headed for the stairs. "Sleep now, and I promise to make your morning worth it."

Levi liked the sound of that. Liked the sound of his quiet house too, knowing it was full of love and family, all thanks to the man beside him. He rose on his toes, brushing his lips over Marsh's. "You make every day worth it. And I can't wait to marry you again."

SIX

LEVI'S PHONE alarm was going off, the never-welcome trilling escalating in volume and pitch, soft to loud, over and over again.

Marsh burrowed into his pillow. "Hit the snooze," he pleaded, needing those extra nine minutes like his life depended on it.

The alarm started another scale.

He rolled from his front onto his side, flinging an arm back the general direction of Levi's torso. And kept rolling, his body meeting no resistance, free-falling all the way to the sheets.

Cold ones at that. Levi had been AWOL from their bed for a while.

Hand to the mattress, Marsh reached out with the other and snagged Levi's phone off the nightstand, finally silencing the dreadful noise. He didn't use to have issues getting out of bed. He was career military and occasionally plagued by the nightmares that came with said career. But more often than not over the past year, he'd slept soundly in his husband's arms, a place he had zero desire to leave in the mornings. Especially when other desires tended to ride him hard first thing. This morning was no different, his dick already half hard, but without Levi in bed beside him, it appeared he was SOL, same as he'd been the last two nights.

Pouting, he tossed Levi's phone back on the nightstand, straightened, and listened for his husband's whereabouts. No other noises coming from inside their primary suite. He listened next for Levi's voice outside their cracked bedroom door. He didn't hear it there either among the others drifting up from the downstairs kitchen with what smelled like sausage gravy and fresh-baked biscuits.

A run with Taco? Late for that, though, the summer temps outside already rising, judging by the sun and heat seeping in from around the edges of the bedroom curtains. Maybe in the backyard under the trellis? Marsh swung his legs off the bed, on his way to peek out the window, when his own phone vibrated. He grabbed it off the charger and read the text from his husband.

In the office.

Texting from the computer, then. Marsh started to type a response when bubbles appeared, Levi typing.

A second text appeared. **Bring the pink bandana. Bedside drawer.**

Marsh's dick perked back up. Stiffened to fully erect when he opened the drawer and found a certain remote sitting atop the strip of pink fabric. Prepped and ready, his husband was apparently feeling frisky this morning. Marsh had admittedly nursed Levi's exhibitionist streak—they'd gotten up to all manner of naughty in front of their big bedroom window that overlooked the Los Peñasquitos canyon—but sex with a house full of people and few walls between them would be a challenge.

One Marsh was up for. His cock too, hard and leaking as he gave it a long, slow stroke.

The bandana would help too. Grabbing it and the remote, he clicked the latter once and imagined Levi's gasp as the vibrations started. Imagined him squirming in his chair, angling the plug's tip for his prostate, rubbing the toy's ridges against his rim, seeking more friction while he waited for Marsh. Who kept him waiting a little longer, brushing his teeth and throwing on sweats and a tee in case anyone from the floor below noticed him crossing the catwalk between the primary suite and the rest of the upstairs rooms.

Thankfully, he reached the home office door unnoticed by everyone but their cat, Burrito weaving around his ankles. He gave the tabby a quick scratch behind the ears, then keyed in the code on the door lock. He slipped inside and closed the door behind him. Levi sat facing the computer, back straight in the task chair they'd recently purchased. It wasn't a particularly comfortable chair on purpose. It kept either of them from sitting in front of the computer for too long.

It was also easier to straddle than a chair with arms.

Or to straddle one's husband in it. Marsh clicked the remote again.

Levi gasped, as needy as Marsh had imagined. And his body—fuck, he was desperate for it already. Eyelids fluttering, Adam's apple bobbing, bare abs clenching as he pressed his ass more firmly down against the seat. Making his cock strain against the front of his athletic shorts, begging for attention, which Levi answered, sliding a hand down his abs and under the waistband, stroking his length. Marsh bit back a moan, admiring the show Levi was putting on for him. Multitasking too, his right hand clicking the mouse and opening windows across Marsh's two monitors. Levi glanced over at him, blue eyes dark with lust and straying to his erection. Darker still. "We have to get this case done before the weekend."

If Marsh could get it done before the next minute, he would. Then he could spend the week doing nothing but fucking his husband between family gatherings. But that was not their reality, this week or any week. He stepped to Levi's side, close enough to feel the heat of his flushed skin, and jutted his chin at the monitor. "Evidence turn up anything?"

Levi continued to open windows across the screen, each a different crime scene photo from Press's place. "Notice anything?"

Squinting, Marsh leaned over Levi's shoulder, trying and failing to see the detail he needed. "Can you zoom in, room by room?"

Levi stretched up and nipped his jaw. "Sorry I made you rush over without your glasses. But you don't need them for this." Before Marsh could capture his lips, Levi scooted forward and gestured at the screen with the hand that had just been in his pants, the tips of his fingers wet with precome.

Marsh grabbed his wrist and held it out to the side, preventing the heathen from touching the screen and keeping temptation out of sight. For now. "Two minutes,"

Marsh grunted. "Two minutes and I will give you what you want." Levi's gaze strayed again to Marsh's cock, and Marsh contemplated whether to continue this conversation at all. In two minutes, he could have Levi out of the chair, the plug out of his ass, and his cock plunging into the hole Levi had stretched open for him.

"What do you see?" Levi said, voice a breathy stutter. He ached with need too, but he was enjoying the anticipation. Same as Marsh. "Look at it as a whole."

Releasing his wrist, Marsh straightened, clicked the plug's vibration up another notch, and forced his gaze to the screen, ignoring the needy keen that slipped past Levi's lips.

As a whole.

Marsh stopped squinting, and that was when he saw it. "Press's office is more trashed than the other rooms."

"Someone was looking for something in there."

"Not his championship ring either."

"Good sign for Press." Levi lifted his ass and shoved down his shorts, cock free to stroke again. "It's more likely about something and someone else."

"Any other evidence?" Marsh asked as he fought the urge to fall to his knees and gag on his husband's cock.

Levi shook his head. "No prints, and nothing else from CSU. Anything off the traffic cams?"

Marsh nudged the chair and Levi over, but before taking control of the keyboard, he dug the bandana out of his pocket and slapped it into Levi's precome-sticky hand. "Gag yourself. We've got a house full of people. Can't have you going all howly when I stuff you full of my cock."

Levi shoved the bandana between his lips, stifling his

immediate groan, then tied it the rest of the way around his neck while Marsh checked the status on the auto and property searches. "Couldn't get the VIN off the car, but we did identify it as a late model, gray Camry. Farmer's pulling all matching registrations in San Diego County. And we'll have property records by ten."

He barely had the last word out when Levi tugged the gag back out of his mouth, yanked Marsh's sweats down, then silenced his needy moans with Marsh's cock instead, swallowing him to the root. It took everything in Marsh not to come right there on the spot. Between the wet, hot suction of Levi's mouth and the sight of him in the mirrored closet doors, cheeks flushed and hollowed, bobbing on his cock while he continued to jerk himself off, Marsh was skating the edge.

As if sensing how close he was, Levi pulled off his cock and stared up at him, only a thin ring of blue around his blown, wide pupils. "My ass feels like a live wire. Need you inside me, now." He shoved the gag back in his mouth and held out an arm for Marsh to haul him up and out of the chair. They switched positions, Marsh claiming the chair and holding Levi's hips so he could admire the vibrating blue plug nestled in his husband's ass. Gorgeous, and all for them. He clasped Levi's cheeks, pulling them apart, then pushing them back together, shifting the plug in the process. "You love this thing, don't you?"

His husband's "more" was a muffled, beautiful thing.

Marsh spread his cheeks and leaned closer, swiping a tongue around the toy's ribbed base and Levi's rim. The scent, the vibrations, Levi's gagged moans were driving him wild, making his cock ache to get in there.

Another couple lashes, then Marsh gave them both what they needed. Holding Levi by one hip, he carefully withdrew the plug and checked with one, two, then three fingers that Levi was slick and ready for him. Satisfied, he lowered Levi onto his cock, legs straddling his lap, back to Marsh's front.

The task chair creaked but held firm. This wasn't their first rodeo in this position, as evidenced by Levi's practiced movements, the up and down of his hips, the turn of his head to meet Marsh's gaze in the mirrored closet doors, the fist he wrapped around his cock.

Marsh covered his hand, working him together, and Levi's gaze was no more, eyes fluttering closed as he rested his head back on Marsh's shoulder, as he bit into the gag each time Marsh thrust up, muffling his grunts. Marsh couldn't tear his eyes from the erotic sight, from the remarkable man in his arms. The one who'd agreed to marry him a year ago and had turned his world upside down. In the best way possible. He'd allowed Marsh to share his home, to get to know his son, and to get to know him, professionally and personally, inside and out. The people and places he loved, the things that made him smile, the touches that made him go wild.

Marsh inched his hand lower and tugged at Levi's balls. "I am the luckiest man alive," he whispered in his husband's ear. "I have the finest piece of ass in all of San Diego sprawled across my lap, riding my cock like he was fucking made for it, and he's also the best person I've ever fucking known." He splayed his left hand over Levi's chest, the rays of morning sun catching his wedding band. Catching Levi's too as he tangled their fingers together.

"And I get to marry you again this weekend. And have a proper"—he thrust up—"fucking"—thrust again—"wedding night."

Levi groaned, strokes coming faster, head thrashing on Marsh's shoulder, his orgasm barreling down on him.

Marsh tightened his grip on his balls. "I'm gonna make it so good for you, baby."

Levi's rhythm began to falter, his body stiffening against Marsh's, muscles coiled tight with tension on the knife's edge of release.

"Open your eyes, Levi. I want you to see us come."

Blue eyes shot open, and Marsh released his balls. Levi's hips jerked, come spilling over their fists, his teeth digging into the bandana as he groaned, long and ragged. Levi falling apart was Marsh's favorite sound. He drew it out, pounding his prostate, heightening the sensation, making Levi's ass clench tight around Marsh's cock as he emptied inside him.

Levi's satisfied pants were another of Marsh's favorite sounds, one of the first that came back to him after their lovemaking. He pulled the gag out of Levi's mouth so he could enjoy the full effect. So he could angle Levi's face in for a kiss, lips brushing in the aftermath of the blinding pleasure that still regularly overtook them. "You're amazing," Marsh whispered.

"My ass is amazing." Levi grinned. "Your cock too."

"And that toy," Marsh said, eyeing the blue plug still vibrating on the floor.

"If my limbs weren't Jell-O, I'd go pick it up."

"We do have to get out of this chair sometime today."

"Boo," Levi said with a pout.

Someone else made the decision for them, twin calls of "Boys!" and "Dads!" echoing from below.

"We're coming!" Marsh shouted back.

"Past tense," Levi muttered, and Marsh lost it, burying his laughter in Levi's neck, squeezing the witty, beautiful man in his arms with all the love his heart would never be big enough to contain.

SEVEN

LEVI WAS STILL RIDING the morning's high as he crossed the FBI bullpen to the conference room, Marsh at his side, his big hand nestled where it belonged at the small of Levi's back. Their lovemaking had been exhilarating—hot, wild, a little naughty—and one hundred percent the connection they'd needed after the past few days. Then after they'd cleaned up and headed downstairs, they'd stolen a few extra minutes with their family over a raucous, delicious breakfast. Between Camilla's and Irina's latest exploits, including *Casseroles for Cows*, a deviously delectable plan for passing a local conservation measure, updates on the goats David had helped deliver last summer, and enough teasing to make poor Brax blush, Levi had left the house with an even wider smile on his face than when he'd first come downstairs.

Days like these, Levi thanked his lucky stars. He'd had it all early on—the love of a good woman, an incredible son, a tight-knit family. Then lost it when cancer had taken David's mother's life. In the aftermath, his heart broken, the rising tide of debt and responsibility drowning him, Levi had drifted from his son, his family, and his friends. And then the cowboy hacker at his side had sauntered into his life and lassoed him out of his misery, helping Levi reconnect with his own family and bringing Levi and David into his. And even working together, Levi never found himself wishing for time away from Marsh. He always wanted more, wanted everything.

Marsh leaned closer as they approached the conference room door. "Wipe that smug grin off your face or everyone is gonna know how hard I railed you this morning."

Levi's cheeks burned, his blush never something he could control, especially around Marsh. "Now they're definitely gonna know."

Turned out there were only two people in the room who might notice—Jamie and Aidan—and both of them were too wrapped up in the folders and papers strewn across the table to even notice they'd entered the room.

Levi cleared his throat. "Good news or bad news?"

"Bit of both," Jamie said, glancing up. "We know why Press got a good deal on the house."

"That's more than we knew yesterday."

"That's the only good part," Aidan said as he stood. "Turns out Press bought a murder house."

"Not exactly," Jamie replied.

"But not far off." Aidan grabbed their mugs and met Marsh by the coffeemaker, spinning up refills while Levi slid into the chair across from Jamie.

"Start from the top," Levi said.

Jamie withdrew a green folder from the rainbow stack to his left and slid it across the table. "Property records. First deed is the one for Press's purchase from Dwight Cousins. Second is from when Cousins purchased the property."

Levi briefly scanned Press's deed; nothing unusual. He flipped to the prior deed. Similarly benign, though the house had been owned in trust. Not an uncommon tax strategy in California. "Eloise Ward signed for the Ward Family Trust. Did she live there?"

"Hold that thought," Jamie said. "Notice anything else?"

Levi flipped back to Press's deed, examining it more closely. Then to Cousins's. All looked in—Wait! He checked the date on Press's, then on Cousins's, surprised at how close they were. "He didn't hold on to it long."

Marsh slid into the chair beside him. "Property values do escalate like magic beanstalks around here." He handed Levi a cup of tea, then scooted back in his chair, nursing his bean water. "Or maybe Cousins was a flipper. Or maybe he was like Agent Kim and couldn't take the planes."

Jamie and Aidan chuckled, Cam no doubt filling them in on his former partner's aversion to the military flyovers that had eventually chased him out of town and up the coast to the LA field office.

Levi sipped his tea and considered Marsh's theories. "The latter is certainly possible. A flipper is possible too, but those improvements at Press's place, while nice, didn't look less than a year old." He set his tea aside and turned his attention back to Jamie. "I'm guessing there's more to the story. Cousins sold the house three hundred and sixty-six days after he bought it, one day past the required holding time for a residential loan."

Smiling, Jamie passed a yellow folder across the table next. "Settlement statements from both transactions."

Marsh whistled from over Levi's shoulder. "Cousins came out of pocket for that delta?"

Aidan nodded. "Tapped his 401K. Penalty is on his tax return."

"Why didn't he just sell it sooner?"

"The lender's penalty was even more exorbitant."

"So he wanted out of that house, bad." Levi spread the papers in front of him and reclaimed his mug, reframing the situation around this latest evidence. "Any issues while he was the owner?"

"Nothing reported," Jamie said. "Checked FBI and the county sheriff's records."

"We need to talk to him," Levi said. "And to the neighbors. There must have been something that chased him out of there."

Marsh made a high-pitched, eerie ghostly noise.

And got a balled-up piece of paper to his face for it, Jamie hitting him square between the eyes. That drew more laughs . . . and tripped something in the back of Levi's mind.

Ghosts.

Dead people.

Ward.

That prior owner's name.

"Tell us about the Ward who lived there before Cousins. Lance Ward, if I remember the news stories correctly?"

Marsh dropped the spooky act, snapping back to professional attention. "News stories?"

"Good memory." Jamie pushed a red folder across the

table to them. "Lance Ward was found dead in the San Elijo Lagoon fifteen months ago."

Levi opened the folder to crime scene photos and was immediately glad he'd gone easy on the sausage gravy and biscuits that morning. Bodies found in water were some of his least favorites. Beside him, Marsh, who'd not gone easy, took one look, then angled his chair away.

"Cause of death was suicide?" Levi asked, closing the folder on the pictures. "I think I remember that too."

Aidan nodded. "Sheriff's department ruled it a suicide officially, but the autopsy was technically inconclusive from the body being in the water too long."

"No one noticed him gone?" Marsh asked.

"Ward was a restauranteur with investments in SoCal and Vegas," Jamie said, as he handed over the last remaining folder, a bulging blue one. "List of restaurants plus his travel and credit card records for the last year of his life are in there. It wasn't unusual for him to be gone long stretches."

"So why did local rule it a suicide?"

Jamie's tone was more somber when he spoke next, the latent investigator's glee taking a back seat to sympathy. "Because he'd tried before. Check the last page in there."

Levi flipped the folder over, then drew out the last sheet, an editorial written by Ward and published in a prominent food magazine. He read the first few paragraphs and was jarred by the contrast between this piece and Ward's ulti-mate fate. "This reads like he came out the other side."

"Doesn't mean he didn't slide back into darkness," Marsh said, and the darkness, the touch of fear in his own voice, had Levi reaching out and laying a hand on his husband's thigh. He'd witnessed Marsh's nightmares over the past year. Infrequent, but there had been enough to know they stayed with Marsh for days after.

"Let's dig into him too," Levi said. "But less about his death and more about his life." He gave Marsh's thigh another squeeze. "Want to show them what we found this morning?"

The thin line of Marsh's mouth curved into a devious smirk, and judging by Aidan's pained "I don't wanna know," he'd noticed this time and made the deduction Levi had expected earlier.

Levi rolled his eyes at his husband. "I can't believe *you* were telling *me* to behave when we walked in here." He snagged the laptop from in front of Marsh and opened the crime scene photos they'd reviewed that morning. He flipped the laptop around but kept it closer to them, aiming for that broader perspective that had helped Marsh realize what he was seeing. "Each room was searched, but when you look at them all together—

"That room," Aidan said, pointing at Press's office, "was searched more thoroughly. Something to do with Ward's work?"

"Or something Ward left behind."

EIGHT

MARSH COULDN'T PARK the RX fast enough once they finally reached their destination in Newport Beach. Catch Me looked like a nice enough place, an upscale eatery on the channel, but Marsh's aching back and legs distracted him from the view. What should've been an hour and fifteen-minute drive had stretched over two and would have stretched longer if Levi didn't seem to know every shortcut in southern California.

The FBI agent waiting for them on the sidewalk in front of the restaurant looked similarly displeased at their delay until he saw Jamie climbing out of the passenger seat. The two were old friends from when Jamie was at MIT, and Matt had been partnered with Jamie's best friend, Cam. "I didn't expect to see you until the weekend," Matt said, LA doing nothing to diminish his New York accent. "What are you doing here early?"

"Matty K," he huffed, hands over his chest, pretending to be injured while doing his best Cam impression. "You don't love me no more?"

"Don't you start with that nickname too!" Smiling, Matt swatted at him once before yanking him into a hug. "Of course I still love you."

Marsh missed having Matt in the San Diego office, the agent briefly partnered with Levi, but from the few times he and Levi had met up with Matt the past year, it was obvious Los Angeles was a better fit for him. "Hope you don't mind the surprise," Marsh said as he took his turn for a hug.

"Not at all, and I don't mind meeting here either." He jutted his chin at the restaurant. "Been meaning to visit this place."

"We're not here to eat, unfortunately," Levi said.

"Doesn't look like we could get a table anyways," Marsh added. All the sidewalk patio tables were full, and a steady stream of summery dressed people continued to go in and out the front doors.

"I didn't mean for the food," Matt said, and the change in his tone from jovial to serious was enough to draw all their glances.

Levi shifted them out of the middle of the sidewalk and off to the side of the patio, out of anyone's earshot. "Explain," he said to Matt. "We're here because the late co-owner was also the owner of a house one of Jamie's former players bought. Had some trouble there the other night."

"Unrelated, I think," Matt said, then turned his attention to Marsh. "Remember that jewel thief case? The one you hacked some info on for me when you were trying to get into my good graces." He tilted his head toward Levi. "And into his pants."

Marsh smirked. "I remember. You still working it?"

"In my spare time. Following the money like we did on the Eder case."

"And it leads here?" Levi asked.

"Maybe. There are some interesting influxes of cash, all coming roughly the same number of days after each theft."

Jamie said the thing they were all thinking. "Laundering."

"That or their funding lines up too perfectly."

Marsh had heard enough to be doubly intrigued now. He removed his hat and gestured toward the door. "Let's go find out."

Matt led the way, having already spoken with the host, not wanting to cause a scene. Good thing as their group looked distinctly too suited for the casual crowd. She led them through the main dining room to a private one behind sliding barn doors. Inside, Luis Rivera, the man they were there to see, sat chatting over empty plates with a white man dressed in entirely too much black for a hot, summer day.

The two men glanced their direction, and Marsh was struck by the stranger in black's appearance, familiar somehow but he couldn't place him. The stranger seemed to place Matt, though, his gaze darting directly to the other agent, same as Matt's had to him. And staying there while the host spoke quietly to Rivera. After a moment, Rivera broke the staredown, sharing a few words with the stranger, then a hug before the man in black disappeared with the host through a door to the kitchen.

"Gentlemen." Rivera gestured them over. "Please, come have a seat."

Levi led the way, hand extended. "Assistant Special

Agent in Charge Levi Bishop." They exchanged friendly handshakes, then each of them in turn, Rivera insisting they call him Luis, before everyone claimed chairs around the table. "Shame I didn't have my son's Remedy album with me," Levi said. "Ryan is his favorite."

That's who the stranger had been—Ryan Lassiter from David's favorite band, Remedy. There was a poster of him in David's room.

"Can't Gino get it signed for you?" Marsh said. "What's the point of having a rock star cousin if you can't call in the occasional favor?"

"Gino Morelli of Middle Cut?" Luis said, his eyes sparkling. "He and Bennett used to be in here all the time. I miss them so much."

"That's them," Levi said with a nod. "And yeah, they've been on tour nonstop these past few years." So much so they'd missed Gino's sister's wedding last year. Only security had shown, not the rock stars.

"Well, if you need Ryan's signature," Luis said, "just let me know."

"How do you two know each other?" Matt asked.

"He was a close friend of Ward's." Luis dipped his chin and crossed himself, muttering a quick prayer for this late friend, before lifting his face and starting again. "Ryan's been a lifesaver. He helped me go through the house after and still drops in whenever the band is in town."

"You and Ward were close too?" Jamie asked.

"We met at a food truck years ago, and by the end of that day, he was my best friend. It was like I'd found the brother I never had. We opened Catch Me together a year later."

"How many concepts have opened together?" Levi said.

"We're"—Luis paused, swallowed hard, then corrected himself—"I'm opening the sixth RW Kitchen concept next month." He ran a shaky hand over his face, then through the tight dark curls on top of his head. "I'm sorry. He's been gone over a year, and I'm still not used to it."

"That's a lot for one person," Marsh said. "We're sorry for your loss."

He dropped his arm, looking sad but resigned. "After what happened, I couldn't let the RWK dream die. That's the last thing he would've wanted."

"After his suicide," Marsh said, skirting the line between question and statement.

Luis's answer was firmly on the side of doubt. "Right."

"You don't seem to believe that," Levi said, picking up on the same skepticism in Luis's voice. Matt and Jamie too, judging by the way they leaned forward in their seats.

Luis pushed back from his, standing. "Can I get anyone a drink?"

They all declined but gave Luis the time he seemed to need. He refilled his glass and stared out the windows at the channel. "I was the one who found him the first time he tried. We'd had back-to-back-to-back failures, concepts that never even made it to opening, and we were losing investors. He always put so much pressure on himself, which was dangerous for someone who suffered from anxiety and depression." He turned away from the water, darkness clouding his expression, his light brown eyes hardening with certainty. "I knew what my best friend looked like, how he acted like during a depressive episode." He shook his head as he sank back into his chair. "This wasn't that. Fuck, we'd just opened our fourth place together and were booked solid. We were on top of the world."

That was consistent with the financials they'd reviewed that morning. Granted, money did not equal happiness, and sometimes success was the worst kind of pressure, but Luis made a convincing case, one that was backed up by years of friendship.

Levi seemed similarly convinced, aiming his questions a different direction. "Had Ward mentioned any issues at his place in Cardiff? Break-ins or anything suspicious?"

"No, nothing. He loved that fucking house, and I'll admit, the view was incredible. But it was also creepy as fuck."

"Creepy?" Marsh asked, keying in on the same isolated vibes he'd picked up there.

Luis's expression darkened once more, but this time the guilt mixed with the pain was unmistakable, from the downturned corners of his mouth to the averted gaze to the blush that hit his brown cheeks. "I once told him that lagoon was the perfect place to hide a body. Still haven't forgiven myself for that joke."

Marsh clasped his shoulder in sympathy, recalling similar comments about desert sand worms eating people whole. And then he'd served there and lost colleagues to the other very real dangers hiding in the sand. No doubt that one jest had been eating Luis up inside every day for the past fifteen months. Probably why Lassiter was checking in on him more too.

"Did Ward have any other enemies?" Jamie asked after

Luis took another sip of water. "Folks who might've wanted to harm him?"

Luis shook his head. "Everyone loved Ward. That's why he ran the front of house operation and I dealt with the kitchens. He was far more of a natural at it."

Marsh didn't doubt that about Ward, but he thought maybe Luis wasn't giving himself enough credit. He'd been the picture of hospitality with them, even as they'd discussed a difficult, painful topic. He wasn't holding anything back. Marsh wondered if he'd been as forthcoming with the local authorities. "Did you go over all this with the sheriff's department at the time?"

Luis nodded, and Levi beat Marsh to the next question. "Did they ever follow up with you?"

"Not once," he said, voice firmer than Marsh had heard it all conversation, bolstered by indignation on behalf of his friend. "They got his medical records, found the scars on his thighs, and had their answer."

Local blowing off another case involving the same house? Or looking the other way, *intentionally*, then and now? Or were they just doing so now to cover their asses from before? As much as their FBI team wanted to stay below the radar with this case, it was becoming more and more clear that they needed to have a conversation with the sheriff's department. And soon.

But first, they needed to finish with Luis, Matt already leading him down the final line of questioning. "How familiar are you with RWK's finances?"

"Intimately, now," he said. "Before, that was Ward's domain. I'm the chef; he was the money and concept guy. It's been a crash course, that's for sure."

Levi withdrew the folded bank records from his coat pocket and pushed the several highlighted sheets in front of Luis. "These are influxes of cash the company received. Do they look familiar to you?"

"Funding rounds," Luis answered without hesitation. "After Ward's death, I had an accountant go over everything and bring me up to speed. I saw those numbers too and was like, woah. I hired someone independent, on Ryan's recommendation. I wanted to be sure it was all legit. The way we'd bounced back after those losses . . ." He smiled, small but proud of what he and his friend had achieved. "It was humbling to know folks in the industry believed in us like that. That they still do." His words got scratchy, thick with emotion, and he cleared his throat before going on. "I've got the backup for everything. I can send over whatever documents you need."

"We'll get you a list," Levi said. "Thank you." He asked around the table for more questions and, hearing none, stood, Marsh and the others following suit. "If you think of anything else," Levi said, handing Luis his card, "that's my number. And Agent Kim is based here in Los Angeles."

Matt handed Luis his card too. "We *will* follow up with you."

Luis thanked them, then slipped into the kitchen, seeking comfort in the familiar, while the host reappeared and led their group back out the way they'd entered. Once outside, Matt let his neutral face fall, the agent looking like he needed some comfort too.

"Sorry we couldn't be of more help on your case," Levi said.

"I'm about to call it cold at this point." Matt said with a shrug. "But I'm glad the visit was useful for yours."

"That's another person who doesn't think it was suicide," Jamie said.

"I tend to believe him," Levi said.

"Well, I can tell you what wasn't cold," Marsh said, cutting a mischievous smirk at Matt. "Those bedroom eyes you and the rock star were giving each other."

"We were not."

Jamie snickered. "You totally were."

Matt looked pleadingly at Levi, who was no help either. "The blush on your cheeks also says you were."

"Something you want to tell us, Matty K?" Jamie needled.

Before he could answer, Marsh's phone rang, the ringtone familiar to three out of the four of them. He drew it out and answered on speaker. "Eagle, what've you got?"

"Local caught wind," she answered, sounding at her annoyed worst. "They're sending over Detective Hines. Get your asses back here, now."

NINE

"WHY ARE you dredging up a cold case?"

Levi was barely off the elevator when the unfamiliar raised voice from the conference room across the bullpen reached his ears.

"And why are there civilians involved?"

Beside him, Marsh cringed. "Guessin' we didn't make it back before Hines made it here."

But someone else had. "Consultants," she corrected, and make no mistake, it was a correction, no matter how sweet and southern Charlotte Henby's voice sounded. "Both of whom had impeccable law enforcement records before moving into the private sector."

"Agent Henby isn't wrong," Kwan added. "Not to mention Lieutenant Colonel Kane's stellar military record."

"Which, from my time working a case here last summer," Charlie said, "I gather is fairly common in San Diego." She smiled as Marsh, Levi, and Jamie entered the room. "Agent Marshall here was career military too. Served with Kane and Kwan, isn't that right?"

"Camp Casey," Marsh said with a shit-eating grin. He tossed his hat on the table, gave Charlie's upturned cheek a kiss, then sank into the chair beside Brax. "Then I worked at the Hague with Agent Henby's husband, who's officiating my wedding this weekend."

"I'm the groom," Levi said as he hugged Charlie on the way to his seat beside Kwan. "And I'm the Assistant Special Agent in Charge here."

The detective's blue eyes bounced around the room, looking for a new target, and landing on Jamie. "You must be the other civilian, then."

"Jameson 'Whiskey' Walker. You may have seen me on television or on the basketball court, as a player or coach." He wasn't one to throw around his fame often, but the way he flashed his cred and camera-ready smile almost made Levi laugh out loud. Jamie slid into the chair beside Aidan and turned the screws some more. "I'm also a former cyber agent, frequent *consultant*, and SAC Talley's husband."

Detective Hines was the physical definition of squirm. Outnumbered, he couldn't figure out which way to go, which way to fire. Levi jumped on the uncertainty. "We have some questions for you, Detective Hines."

Marsh leaned forward, picking up the thread. "Like why you didn't more thoroughly investigate the break-in at Presley Jackson's house this past weekend?"

On the defensive, Hines remained standing, his height above them an illusion of power his white knuckles on the chair back gave away. "No reason to think it was anything more."

"Why did you think it was anything less?" Levi countered. "The current owner is a professional basketball player. A prior owner of the same house was murdered."

"Committed suicide."

"We'll get to that."

"Nothing was taken."

"Exactly," Jamie said. "Including Press's championship ring, which was sitting out in the open on his desk, the most trashed room in the entire house if you'd bothered to look."

"And not just any house," Levi continued. "A multi-million-dollar one in Cardiff. Where someone died fifteen months ago."

"We talked to his business partner earlier today," Marsh said. "Doesn't sound like you investigated that case either."

"Look, he had a history—"

"What?" Levi cut in. "You assumed because he had a mental health condition and had attempted suicide in the past that it was the same this time? That Mr. Ward just threw himself into that lagoon?" He had seen cases, detectives like this before. More often in the human trafficking context, where asshole detectives like Hines wanted to make it the victim's fault, but in either case, it pissed Levi off to see someone's life and their death so easily dismissed. Especially by officers sworn to protect people and to solve their deaths or disappearances.

Cornered, Hines stepped back and raised his hands, palms out. "Look, no harm no foul. In either case. We got a board full of more pressing matters. This wasn't anything. Either time."

"Then you won't mind us investigating," Kwan said, having Levi's back, like she always did.

"Why do you care about a random B&E?"

"The current owner is a former player of mine," Jamie answered. Hines's wide eyes were further proof he hadn't given this case a second thought. Clearly not a minute of research.

"You don't have an interest," Kwan added. "We do."

"Fine." Hines shrugged. "Have at it. One less case on my board."

"I'll have the paperwork over to you by the end of the day," Levi said while mentally calculating the jurisdictional hoops needed to paper it. They'd figure it out, probably before Hines, who was already halfway across the bullpen, would give it a third thought.

"Well," Levi said, turning back to the table. "I don't think the sheriff's department was purposely covering anything up."

"Agree," Brax said. "This just doesn't rank on their priority ladder." And the former police chief would know, having had to manage a ladder like that before.

"And ours?" Levi asked his boss, confirming the front she put on for Hines was gonna stick.

"Same answer as before," she said, standing. "It's your week off. If this is how you want to spend it, go for it." She paused over the threshold, giving them the same warning she had yesterday. "Just be done by Friday."

"Seems to be a trend," Levi said once she was out of earshot. "David gave us the same ultimatum."

Knowing them well, Charlie grinned. "Who are you more afraid of? Kwan or your kid?"

Levi glanced at his husband; they answered together. "David."

TEN

MARSH CRUISED in from the back patio with the last of the empty platters and grilling utensils, savoring the AC and the relative quiet of the kitchen. Outside, the cookout was still in full swing, family and friends from one end of their backyard to the other, chatting with one another and dancing to the music playing on the outdoor speakers. "How are we gonna fit even more people here on Saturday? Our neighbors are gonna kill us. Maybe we should call Aunt Liz and see if we can do it at the mansion."

"We're doing it here," Levi said as he warmed up the espresso machine for after-dinner drinks and desserts. "We'll just send Jamie to the neighbors with a smile and a pint of barbecue."

Marsh filched a few bits of pulled pork from the chafing tray and popped them in his mouth. "Not a bad plan." He wished their other plans for the week had gone better, but Press's case still wasn't wrapped yet. Granted, having Jamie here early to contribute to the gut-busting picnic was a plus, but Marsh was worried about the stress Levi was putting on himself, juggling work and family and more visitors by the day. It was good they'd had this cookout scheduled for tonight. It was a break Levi couldn't get out of and the breather they all needed after pushing hard the past three days.

"So, I was thinking," Levi started, and Marsh figured he knew what was next. His husband, agent extraordinaire and certified workaholic, was not done pushing. "Maybe I should—"

Stepping behind him, Marsh twined his arms around his waist and nipped his neck, cutting off the return-to-work comment Levi was about to make. "Maybe you should take the night off and spend it with your friends and family."

"But Press doesn't have a place to go home to."

Marsh slid the tamper out of his hand, clicked the portafilter into place, then clicked the Start button before turning his husband in his arms. "Does it look like Press is having a bad time?" Marsh flicked a glance out the back windows to where Press was at one end of the patio table, animatedly talking with Jamie, Farmer, Trevor, and David, who'd remained in his crush's orbit since he'd walked in the door. "Last I passed by them, they were laying odds for preseason number one. If Press can take a night off from studying and his murder house, so can you."

Marsh leaned forward and captured his husband's lips, pleased when Levi relaxed into the kiss, the two of them lazily making out until the portafilter gurgled.

Levi drew back but not far, resting his head against Marsh's shoulder. "Thank you for always pulling me back from that edge. It's just tough when there are so many moving pieces and so much evidence but none of it connects."

While they hadn't solved the case yet, Aidan and Brax had turned up more clues in their interviews with Cousins and the neighbors, and they were continuing to turn up leads on Ward too. As Levi said, they just needed to find the piece that tied it all together.

But not tonight. Tonight was for them and their family, all of them gathered to get a jump start on the celebration of their love, all of them instrumental in nurturing that love into what it was today. The most important connection of Marsh's life. He palmed his husband's cheek, thumb skating across his sun-warmed skin. "I love how hard you work, how good you are at your job, and this is part of mine, as your husband."

"It's appreciated." Levi lifted his chin and met his gaze. "I just want this done by Friday so we can fully enjoy ourselves."

"Oh, I intend to fully enjoy every minute of our wedding weekend and every inch of you on our wedding night."

"Then we gotta finish this case."

"Which is why," he said, kissing the tip of Levi's nose, "we're gonna make your mother's affogato." Marsh paused because after a year, he knew what was coming in three, two, one . . .

"Levi, Marsh, where's my dessert?"

Levi lost it, falling against his chest in a fit of giggles, the sound one hundred percent welcome, one of Marsh's favorites.

"On its way!" Marsh shouted back, then to Levi, leaned

down and spoke next to his ear. "Which is why we're gonna serve our guests dessert, we're gonna spend some more time with them, and then while you spend some time with your son and family tonight, I'm going to do some hacking." Levi lifted his head, mouth open to object, and Marsh kissed him quiet. "You put in the extra time the other morning. Now it's my turn."

"Are you sure?"

Marsh laced their fingers together, their wedding bands catching the evening light streaming into the canyon. "As sure as I am that I can't wait to marry you again in front of all these people and more on Saturday."

ELEVEN

WHILE LEVI GOT to spend the rest of the evening with his family, he and Marsh were up and out of the house before sunrise, called back to Press's place by an early morning security alarm, a glass break set off on the lower level. On alert this time, Hines apparently taking them seriously, a sheriff's deputy was already on-site when they arrived. He'd done a complete look around and saw no evidence that the burglar had made it inside. Only broken the lower-level window, then fled when the alarm had sounded.

Levi asked the deputy to keep watch outside while he and Marsh checked inside, clearing each room, confirming what the deputy suspected. No one had been inside the house, the alarm doing its job. Levi texted the deputy that he was off guard duty, then slid onto a metal stool at the dining bar beside Marsh. "They're still after something here."

"Yep." Marsh angled his phone toward Levi, footage from the traffic cam displayed. "Different car this time." A light-colored Prius. "Probably another rental, but I'll have Farmer run it. This time of morning, there's nothing else around. That's gotta be them."

The gray car Press had spied had been a dead end. So had all the other maybe-suspect-cars that the neighbors and Cousins recalled. No one car was the same and not all were caught on camera, the stoplight only recently installed. Of those on camera, some were rentals, some were owned by local folks, and a fair few belonged to real estate agents. No one with a rap sheet.

Levi drummed his fingers on the stainless steel bar top, counting the bright, multicolor backsplash tiles of the kitchen as he cycled through possibilities in his head. He kept coming back to the same ones. "It has to be something in the walls, ceiling, or floor. Or in a panic room–type space."

Marsh shook his head. "Cousins looked for the latter."

While he, Marsh, and Jamie had been in Newport Beach the other day, Aidan and Brax had questioned Cousins. The prior homeowner had thought this place would be his dream home; it had turned into a nightmare. Hang-ups, drive-bys, lights in windows late at night, unexplained power and Wi-Fi outages. Cousins had worked from home, leaving little opportunity for break-ins, but he'd had the sense someone was always watching for the opportunity. He couldn't handle constantly looking over his shoulder, being uncomfortable in the place he spent most of his time. He'd wanted out, no matter the cost.

Marsh tapped again at his phone, bringing up the floor plans. "I don't see anything here like a panic room or secret space." Levi leaned in, peering over his shoulder, as Marsh spread his fingers, zooming in room by room, spending extra time on the in-home office.

"Me neither," Levi said. "All the corners and dimensions line up. What about the floors, walls, or ceiling?"

"CSU didn't find anything up or down. As for the walls, short of busting into them, we can't know for sure. But—"

"The break-in didn't go that far either," Levi said, following Marsh's train of thought. The place had been tossed but not destroyed. A matter of time? Or if it wasn't in the floors, walls, or ceiling—whatever *it* was—was it in something that had been removed? Without the burglar's knowledge? "Do we have the sales contract to Cousins? And the one to Press?" Marsh nodded, scrolling once more. "We need the Bills of Sale. What carried all the way through?"

"Looks like most of it," Marsh said after a moment. "Couch."

"Tossed."

"Beds."

"Shredded. What about in the office?" Levi said, sliding off his stool and heading in that direction, Marsh on his heels. He stepped into the smallish room, took a moment to admire the view out these windows too, then rotated toward Marsh, who'd posted up against the doorjamb. "All right, what've we got?"

"Desk."

"Glass." The one intact piece of furniture left in here.

"Chair."

"Leather," Levi said, spinning it. "Cut."

"Rug."

"Rolled up." Shoved against the wall. Against the—

"Wall art."

He gestured at the broken frame propped on the rug. "Also ripped."

"Well, this is curious."

Levi spun to face his husband. "What is?"

"There was a wine fridge on the bill of sale to Cousins," Marsh said, straightening off the doorjamb. "But it was crossed out. Initialed by Cousins and LR."

"Luis Rivera? He removed it?"

Marsh had already dialed, the call ringing on speaker, by the time Levi reached his side. "Hello," Luis answered, sounding surprisingly awake for five in the morning. And somewhere surprisingly noisy. Near the water, judging by the boat horns and seagulls in the background.

"Luis, this is Agents Bishop and Marshall, we're sorry to call so early."

"Best time of the day to buy fish," he replied. "Give me just a second." They listened as he negotiated a halibut purchase, then after a moment, the background noise quieted, Luis having moved out of whatever hustle and bustle he'd been in. "What can I help you with, agents?"

"Did Ward use to have a wine fridge in his office?" Levi asked.

"Oh, yes," Luis replied. "Eloise was going to sell it to the buyer, but I wanted it for the underbar in one of the restaurants. We worked out a deal."

"Did you notice anything unusual? About the fridge?"

"No. It worked fine. Some junk behind it when we moved it out, but Ward wasn't the neatest guy."

"What kind of junk?"

"Receipts for restaurant supplies. A couple of flash drives."

Marsh's eyes grew wide. "Did you check the flash drives?"

"Gibberish," Luis said. "Just a single file on each. A random string of numbers."

Marsh hit the Mute button. "They're passkeys to other files." He took the phone off mute, asking Luis, "Any chance you also have Ward's laptop?"

"I do, since he only had his RWK one. I've got it in secure storage with the rest of the work files we cleaned out of the house. Backup in case I needed to access anything."

"Can you text us the address and meet us there?" Levi said. "I know it's early—"

"I want to know what happened to my friend," Luis said. "I'll text you the address. It's here in Newport Beach."

"This time of morning, we can be there in an hour."

"I'll see you then."

"And Luis," Marsh added, "bring the flash drives."

TWELVE

THEY COULD HAVE WAITED for the searches to come back on the entities revealed in the encrypted files Marsh, Jamie, and Farmer had cracked with the passkeys from Luis. But Levi—and Luis—had ultimately made the call to accelerate matters.

Levi, because they were coming up fast on their David-Kwan Friday deadline. Luis, because he wanted to know who Ward was laundering money for.

While thankfully not through the company accounts, Ward had been using RWK's connections with suppliers to buy equipment, food stuffs, and other goods at an industry discount. With dirty money. Ward would then sell those goods on the secondary market and get paid in clean money that was funneled back to his client. A misadventure Ward had entered into during that period of failures—when he'd spiraled and tried to take his life to escape the pressure and his own bad decisions. But then things had turned around and Ward had wanted out of the laundering business.

At least that was the story Marsh had deduced from the invoices and notes Ward had left in his encrypted files. The pieces all fit, including Ward's dead body in the lagoon and the launderers' desperation to clean up after themselves. To find the evidence they'd thought was still in the house but which had been unintentionally removed by Luis.

"You don't have to do this," Levi had told Luis earlier that afternoon. "We can take it from here. At this point, they don't even know you have the information they're after."

"You don't have to put yourself in danger," Marsh had added. He liked Luis. Respected how forthcoming and cooperative he'd been through all this. He was an innocent wrapped up in Ward's mess; he didn't have to put his life or business on the line.

"I need to do this for myself," Luis had replied, voice thick with tears but no less adamant for it. "And for Ward." He still had his friend's back, even knowing what he'd done, even with Ward gone. Marsh respected him more for it. A deep breath later, he'd placed the call to the number on the invoices and left the message they'd rehearsed with him. "Hello. This is Luis Rivera. Ward's old business partner. I have the information you've been looking for. I'm interested in learning more."

It was a believable enough scenario—that Luis had come into possession of the incriminating evidence and wanted to revive the arrangement. A return text had arrived ten minutes later—a time later that evening and an address.

Which was how Marsh found himself between Jamie and Brax, in front of the monitors of the mobile command van. They were parked across the street from an industrial complex in Oceanside, waiting for the launderers to arrive for a seven o'clock meeting with Luis. Between them and the meeting site were four lanes of rush hour traffic and a steady stream of folks going to and from the complex. Organized in a U-configuration, the complex's three buildings were each a single story, four suites each, roll-up bay doors at the front of each unit. All but one of the units had their doors rolled down, tenants wisely staying cool in the sweltering heat.

Marsh would bet Levi was already sweating through his shirt under his tactical vest, positioned as he was in the lookout spot on the roof of the complex's center building. He'd wanted to be one of the primary tactical teams, but Marsh had pulled him aside and, admittedly unfairly, reminded him that David would be supremely pissed if Levi got shot two days before the wedding and had to delay it again. Levi had cursed Marsh's sudden but inevitable betrayal and conceded the primary posts, taking lookout instead.

"Teams report," he called, getting "Clear" replies from Farmer's team in the first unit of the right-side building and from Aidan's team in the center building, one unit over from where the meet would go down.

Charlie's "Incoming" from where she was circulating among other FBI agents pretending to be civilians at a company picnic at the far end of the left building drew Levi's bird's-eye view her direction.

His camera caught a gray Camry pulling into the parking lot, driving past the picnic area, and into a spot near the middle building. "Looks like a match," Jamie said.

"Same make and model as the car Press identified the night of the break-in."

"Talley, you're up," Marsh said.

"Eyes on," Aidan confirmed.

Two white men climbed out of the car. The driver was middle-aged, suited, and carried himself with an air of authority. The passenger was younger, a bruiser who walked a step behind Mr. Suit on their way to the unit Luis waited out front of. Marsh would bet his Stetson that Bruiser was the person who'd trashed Press's home Saturday night. Fit the description, same as the car.

"Mr. Rivera," the suited man greeted, his words audible through the in-ear comm Luis wore. "Dayton McConnell," he said, hand extended.

"Run him," Marsh said to Jamie and Brax, the former checking all the sources, legit and otherwise, available to him, the latter on rap sheets and records. "Fifty-fifty shot it's an alias."

"I was surprised to hear from you," McConnell said.

"I was surprised to learn what Ward was up to," Luis replied.

"Were you?"

"He didn't let on. Shame, as I might have been able to help."

"I'd like to hear how," McConnell said. "*If* you have what I need."

Luis nodded, and McConnell gestured toward the door. Bruiser keyed in a code on the lock pad, and the group entered, disappearing from view.

"Farmer, Henby, second position," Levi said, moving

their teams closer, the three teams now surrounding the unit, Levi maintaining lookout.

"How do you think you can help us, Mr. Rivera?"

Luis didn't reply immediately, and Marsh's heart lodged in his throat, fearing the worst for a moment, until Luis finally spoke again. "Are you in the tortilla business? This is a lot of masa."

Marsh pointed at Brax. "Check for orders in Ward's invoices. Do we have Ward buying the masa with dirty money?" Then to Jamie. "See if—"

"If it was sold on the secondary," Jamie said, following. "On it."

Marsh tuned back into the conversation, shifting between camera views, monitoring for any additional activity.

"We lost our best trader," McConnell said. "Product stalled."

"Lost or fired?" Luis countered.

"He wasn't adhering to company policy."

"Levi?" Marsh prompted.

"Hold," he answered. "Not enough yet."

Marsh wanted to say something to Luis, to provide him some encouragement; they were so close, but the chef had elected not to go two-way on the comms, afraid he might give away the op with his reactions.

"Got the masa," Brax said. "Ward purchased it two days before his death."

"Haven't found it sold yet, but McConnell's an alias," Jamie said. "Real name is Joseph Gallagher. Specializes in laundering money for white-collar criminals. Explains the Brioni suit."

A few quick keystrokes after that, Brax chimed in. "Got him. Was operating out of Chicago until he moved west two years ago. LAPD and SD Sheriff have both brought him in for questioning, multiple times."

"I need assurances," Luis said to Gallagher. "None of this can get back to RWK."

"We had the same agreement with Mr. Ward. We'll honor that, *if* you have what we're looking for."

"Flash drives." Luis clicked them together twice, the signal they'd agreed on.

"Talley, Henby," Levi said. "First position. Farmer, hold." The moment Luis handed over those flash drives, he would be at his most vulnerable, no longer of use to Gallagher. The tactical teams had to be ready to act.

"These contain all of Ward's invoices and records," Luis said, as they'd also rehearsed. "The dirty money you sent him, what he bought, what he sold, and the clean money he returned. This is what you need?"

"Are there any other copies?"

"None. I didn't figure that would win me any business."

"The masa was sold," Jamie said. "But neither the product nor the money was delivered. Holy shit."

"What?" Marsh said, whipping his gaze to him.

Jamie dragged a phone log onto the middle monitor, a row highlighted. "Ward called the sheriff's department with a tip the night before he was killed. They never called him back."

"So *that's* why local is so determined to ignore this," Marsh said.

"And that's why Ward was killed," Levi said. "Final straw."

"And now," Brax said, "the cops are gonna ignore it again to cover their own incompetence and a leak."

"At the expense of Press's safety," Farmer chimed in. "*Fuck* that."

His vehemence almost distracted Marsh from the conversation still going on the other end of the comm. "I can move this masa by tomorrow," Luis said. "I can move more."

"All right, Mr. Rivera. If the money is in the accounts by tomorrow morning, we can work together."

"And if it's not?"

"Then you'll be fired too."

"Talley, Henby, go!" Levi ordered. "Farmer, back up!"

Chaos erupted over the comms, Marsh watching as FBI agents streamed into the unit, catching Gallagher and Bruiser off guard, Aidan and Charlie taking them down before they could draw the weapons they were carrying, and giving the rest of the agents time to form a wall around Luis.

By the time Levi made it down from the roof and into the unit, Gallagher and Bruiser were in cuffs and being read their rights.

"You got what you need?" Luis asked him.

"We did," Levi said. "And we couldn't have done it without you."

"Without Ward," Luis said with a nod for his friend. "In the end, he gave us what we needed."

He had. Case closed with explanations about more than one aspect of the case.

But not the most unexpected explanation of the week. That came with Farmer charging into the unit, stalking directly up to Bruiser, and slugging him with a right hook. "That's for wrecking my boyfriend's new place." Then kicked him with his metal foot. "And that's for scaring the shit out of him."

"Something you want to tell us, Farmer?" Levi said, and Marsh could hear the grin in his voice, could see it through the body cam on Farmer's gear.

"Yeah," he said, not bothering to hide his own smile. "My plus one for the wedding is Press. Hope that's not a problem."

"Not at all," Marsh said, Levi completing his sentence, "We'll see you both on Saturday."

THIRTEEN

INFORMAL ATTIRE HAD BEEN the right call. Levi couldn't imagine a better sight than his husband standing before him on their second wedding day in his snow-white Stetson, red-checked shirt, shiny belt buckle, and faded jeans.

Mount Cowboy in all his glory.

"You were wearing the same outfit the day I met you," Levi said, voice raised so their guests packed into the back-yard could hear him. "I was at one of the lowest points in my life, and this mountain of a cowboy swaggered into my world and turned it upside down." Not everyone in the group was privy to the full story, so Levi kept the details vague even as his mind rewound to that night. Replayed Marsh sliding into the chair across from him, wearing that same outfit and a too-attractive smirk, telling Levi to *Marry me*. "And when you proposed, you told me the only answer you needed was *yes*."

Levi had said yes that night a year ago to a marriage of convenience. Today he was saying yes to so much more.

He wrapped both of Marsh's hands in his. "Yes, Emmitt Marshall, to spending every day of the rest of my life with you. Yes to raising our son together." Beside Levi, David groaned in true teen fashion, and Levi amended, "To the extent he lets us. Yes to all the family and friends you've added to our lives." Cheers and applause rippled across the yard. "And yes to the love and laughter you fill my world with every day. Yes to everything with you."

Marsh dipped his chin and lifted his hands in Levi's, bringing Levi's knuckles to his lips. He brushed a kiss over them, then righted his gaze, the shiny gleam to his eyes making Levi's water too.

"I knew you were the one the minute I laid eyes on you, Levi Bishop, and not just because you look like a fucking pinup model."

"Language," David and Lily chirped together, loud enough to be heard over the rest of their guests' laughter.

Levi chuckled too, shaking a few tears loose that Marsh wiped away. He left his hand on Levi's cheek, cradling it in that way that made Levi feel cherished, that had obliterated the loneliness at a time when that was all he'd been able to see.

"Then I got to know you," Marsh went on. "I learned you were a good man, a good father and son, a good brother and friend, and a damn good agent. I watched you struggle and fight for those you love and what you believe. I worked by your side as you rescued those in need and saved god only knows how many more people." He brushed more of Levi's tears away, then lifted and joined their hands again, over his chest. "I fell in love with the best man I've ever met, one I'm lucky to wake up next to and work beside each day, and I will spend the rest of our lives trying to live up to your example. I will do whatever it takes to earn each and every one of those yeses."

There were more than a few sniffles in the crowd, one even from Levi's side, though Levi would never call his son on it because he was losing the battle himself. Marsh's words, his admiration and love, meant everything to him. He'd found a partner in all aspects of his life.

Sean, Charlie's and Trevor's husband and Marsh's other best friend, likewise needed to clear his throat before picking back up with the ceremony. "Do we have the rings?" he asked in his officiant role.

Beside Marsh, Brax lowered Lily to the ground, and she scurried in front of Sean with the basket Camilla and Irina had helped her make. The platinum and rose gold bands Levi and Marsh had worn the past year shone bright in their bed of bougainvillea, picked fresh from their yard's abundance that morning.

Levi plucked out the larger of the two bands and slipped it onto Marsh's finger. "Take this ring," Levi said, "as a promise that I will always bring my heart home to you." Words he'd spoken, a pledge he'd made in a Salzburg hotel room a year ago. He'd kept that promise then. Would keep it for the rest of his life.

Snagging Levi's ring from the basket, Marsh kissed the top of Lily's head, then turned back to Levi and slid the ring onto his finger. "Take this ring as a promise that I will always bring my heart home to you."

Cheers erupted, Lily's and David's the loudest. So loud Levi almost missed the words he'd been most eager to hear all ceremony. "By these promises made," Sean said, "and by the good fortune of being your friend, I pronounce you husband and husband. Again. Now kiss, because we all know you're dying to."

Levi didn't have to be told twice, claiming Marsh's lips and tasting the promise of forever in his husband's smile.

FOURTEEN

MARSH WAS MIXING two Manhattans at the kitchen island when David and Levi came bustling in, Taco on their heels, the greyhound scouting for any dropped bits from the serving trays they carried. Too bad for him; the plates on Levi's tray were wiped clean and David's candy cane–striped bucket of ice was empty of its frozen delights.

"Sorry, buddy," Marsh said, scratching behind the dog's velvety soft ears. "You'll have to settle for a biscuit." He tossed one into the great room and Taco sprinted after it, Marsh closing the gate behind him. Better to keep him out of Levi's and David's way, the latter of whom was sweating through his Grinch tee and had his head in the freezer.

"Your ugly Christmas sweater didn't last long," Marsh teased.

"Because it's pushing ninety out there."

"You could've not—"

"Nope," David said, whipping around with another armful of ice pops that he dumped into the chilled bucket. "You promised me a Christmas wedding. You and Dad might have wanted to go all cowboy, I get it, but I had all this Christmas shi—supplies—to go through." He gestured at the bucket, then at the breakfast table covered in holiday-themed plates, cups, and napkins. Even the utensils had little Christmas trees on the end.

"It is July first," Levi said, finishing up at the sink. He dried his hands and circled the island to Marsh's side. "It was either Christmas in July or wait until December."

"And risk you delaying it again?" David squawked. "No way in hell. Or more like Christmas in hell. I mean July. No objections!"

"Well, mark this date in history," Marsh said as he handed a glass to Levi, then clinked his own against it, the both of them chuckling.

David rolled his eyes, hard, then with an indignant huff picked up the ice bucket. "I may just keep all of these for myself."

"You're not gonna share with Trevor?" Marsh teased, and David gave an even harder eye roll. "Oh-hoh, what's that about?"

"He tried to convince me to add more Shakespeare to my summer reading list. The thrill is gone."

"I know you know he's an English lit professor."

He flitted a hand in the air, then with a spin of his heel, cruised back outside, humming B.B. King melodies under his breath.

"He's having fun, right?" Marsh asked Levi once David was out of earshot. He and David poked at each other mercilessly, but his son's happiness was as important as Levi's, two sides of the same coin.

Levi smiled, the fondness for his son radiating. "He's having a blast. We gave him what he wanted."

"And you?"

All that fondness shone Marsh's direction. "There's nothing else I want right now. Except maybe a kiss."

Marsh obliged, leaning down for a slow, soft brush of their lips, the spicy rye and cherry sweetness delicious on Levi. Same as the outfit he'd worn today. Marsh loved his man in suits, but he loved him like this too. In a short-sleeved chambray with red and white stripes that showed off his biceps and hugged his back, jeans that likewise hugged his ass, and cowboy boots that had become well-worn over the past year. Marsh's black Stetson had been a surprise; he'd figured Levi would've worn his white one too.

"Why this one?" Marsh asked, bumping a knuckle against the brim.

"I love the white one you got me, and I love the white one on you," he said, bumping back against Marsh's brim. "But this black one . . . I remember you wearing it that first day we were in Texas, when you rode out with Camilla." Levi laid a hand over his chest. "It hurt here. I knew then I was in trouble."

"I was so gone for you by then," Marsh confessed, then dove in for another kiss. He would never get enough of this amazing man. Was ready to—

A throat cleared behind them, and they parted to find Farmer and Press just inside the doorway. Hands clasped, they stood close, same as they'd been all afternoon, the two adorably inseparable, clearly smitten with each other. More than smitten if Press had bought a house here in San

Diego and was making post-ball-career plans to be near Farmer.

"You guys having a good time?" Marsh asked as he rested against the island.

"You know how to throw a party," Farmer said with a wide grin. "And it's good to be around people like us, in lots of ways."

Marsh loved working with the guy—he was a hell of a hacker—but this meant even more. Providing a safe, uplifting space where folks could be themselves and see themselves in others. His family, Levi's family had made a point of it, and they were always happy to open their arms to more. "We'll have to make more of a habit of it, yeah? Whenever Press is here in SD."

"We'd like that," Press said. "I also wanted to say thanks again for all the help this week. And I'm sorry for not telling you about us upfront. When Jamie said he knew some folks in San Diego who could help, I didn't think it would be you two who'd show up at the house. Threw me for a bit of a loop."

Farmer bumped his shoulder. "You got the best."

"I'm grateful," Press said. "For your help and to know Jermaine has such good people around him."

"We're lucky to have him too," Levi said. "And I'm glad you'll be back in your house soon."

"Me too," Press said.

The launderers had been arrested and booked, a formal inquiry opened at the sheriff's department, Luis cleared of all involvement, and by tomorrow afternoon, Press's place would be good as new, courtesy of the Madigan cleanup magic.

"It's a lovely place," Marsh said.

"We thought so," Farmer replied, and Marsh would be shocked as shit if the two weren't moved in together there by the end of the summer.

They exchanged a few more words, then after a round of hugs, Press and Farmer wandered back to the party, leaving Marsh and Levi in the kitchen, finishing their drinks to the sound of their friends and family laughing and having a good time, enjoying the wedding day Levi deserved.

That Marsh was so very happy to give to him. But right then, Marsh wanted to give him something else more.

"So . . ." he drawled at Levi's ear. "How long do we have to stay at our own party before it's acceptable to sneak out? Because as much as I love this, I'd love to fuck my husband more."

Levi kept him in suspense for the two minutes it took to finish their drinks, to take their glasses to the sink, and to wash them out. When he returned to Marsh's side, he took his hand, kissed his knuckles with a sly smirk, then spun on his heel as fast as their son had earlier and bolted for the garage door, dragging a laughing, head over heels in love Marsh behind him.

FIFTEEN

THE LAST TIME Levi stood in this hotel room, his world had been spinning out of control. *A circus*, he'd thought that day as he'd gazed out the balcony doors at the ocean. The seventy-two hours since Emmitt Marshall had swaggered into his life had been a dizzying blur, and that afternoon, an hour before their first wedding, the tilt-a-whirl had been on max speed. Until Marsh had offered him a ring and his help.

Had begged him to take it.

Levi's world had stopped spinning. Sure, there'd been other dizzying moments on that first case together and in the year since, but standing here today, gazing out the same open patio doors at the moonlit ocean, Levi had never felt steadier.

Marsh stepped behind him, his chest warm against Levi's back, his arms twining around his waist, holding him close. "I hope it's okay I brought you here tonight."

"It's perfect." He laced his fingers with Marsh's, their rings softly pinging as they slotted next to each other. "I was just thinking how much has changed." He leaned his head back on Marsh's shoulder. "How steady you made my world."

"You made it that way, Levi." Marsh kissed his temple and squeezed him tighter. "You had the courage to say yes, to risk everything and trust me when you had no reason to. You're remarkable, baby."

"So are you. You put yourself out there, saw a person in need, a way to save me and so many others, and you went for it. You always go for it." Levi turned in his arms and coasted his hands up Marsh's chest, the heat beneath the cotton warming his palms. "I'd say we both won."

"Best play," Marsh said with a smile. "In chess terms."

Levi chuckled. "If you say so." No matter how many hours he spent on the periphery of Marsh's games with David or Brax, chess would never be Levi's forte. But he did occasionally pick up terms. "*I'd* say romantic chess is more in order. Sudden attacks and sacrifices, if I recall correctly?"

"You do," Marsh said with a smirk.

Levi curled his hands in Marsh's shirt and yanked, the pearl buttons unsnapping, baring Marsh's golden bronze skin to Levi's hands and lips. He spread the shirt wider, fingers sneaking under the lapels, teasing his nipples, while he kissed across his collarbone, into the hollow of his throat, and down between his pecs.

Marsh hissed and cupped the back of his head, fingers carding through his hair. "What about the sacrifices?"

"Do forty-year-old knees count?"

Marsh laughed out loud, the sound going straight to Levi's heart—and his dick.

He wanted—needed—his husband.

Levi sank to his knees. A sacrifice, but not as painful as it could have been thanks to the hotel carpet, and the second he got Marsh's flush, erect cock out of his jeans, Levi forgot all about his aging joints. Leaning forward, Marsh's cock brushing his cheek, he nuzzled the crease between his thigh and groin, savoring the heat and musk of Marsh's skin. He inhaled deep, then traveled a path designed to tease and torment, his lips teasing Marsh's balls, his tongue swiping over his taint, before he buried his nose in the crease on the other side of his cock.

"Jesus, Wolfy, you're killing me." Marsh tangled a hand in his hair, then slid it lower, palming one side of his cock, pressing the long, hard length against Levi's cheek. "You feel how hot I am for you? How much I want you?"

Groaning, it was all Levi could do not to give in and take Marsh in his mouth, to taste all that heat and the salty precome he could smell. He executed another swift attack instead, hands diving over Marsh's hips and spreading his cheeks. Marsh preferred to top, but his needy grunts whenever Levi swirled a finger around his rim were intoxicating. Made his own hole clench to be filled.

"I see you squirming," Marsh said from above him. "Like you did in that chair the other morning. You need it, don't you? My cock inside you, filling you up, making that hole mine."

"Please," Levi whimpered into the wiry hair at the base of Marsh's cock.

"It is now. All the yeses you said in front of our friends and family today. You made it official. Your heart and your hole are mine."

Finally giving in, Levi licked a slow stripe along the

underside of Marsh's cock and, when he reached the tip, swirled his tongue. He opened his eyes and locked gazes with Marsh's dark, heated one. "Take it, then."

If Levi thought his moves were bold and sweeping, they were nothing compared to Marsh yanking him up off the floor, ripping open his shirt, and tossing him onto the bed, Marsh's big body covering his in the blink of an eye.

But then Marsh stilled, a hand on his cheek, gaze intense as he stared down at him. "I'm yours too. Never forget that. I dirty talk and dominate because I know that's what you need, but make no mistake, you own all of me, Levi Bishop, heart and soul. I will do whatever it takes to earn every one of your yeses."

Tears threatened, probably would have fallen again, if Marsh hadn't cupped him through his jeans and stroked. Eyes rolling back in his head, Levi surrendered to Marsh taking control of his body. Taking him apart piece by piece, as he proved his words. Every kiss down his neck and across his chest, every lick and suck of his cock, every lash of his tongue over Levi's hole. All of it exactly what Levi needed, all of Marsh's energy and attention focused on him, imparting all of that love to him.

Earning every *Yes*.

"Yes" as Marsh thrust inside him.

"Yes" as he wrapped a hand over Levi's around his cock, the two of them stroking him together.

"Yes" as they rocked and climbed and came together, Marsh filling him and Levi spilling over their fists.

"Yes" as they sank to the bed after, their tangled bodies spent.

"Yes" as Marsh whispered words of affection in his ear,

promises of a future full of days and nights like the one today, full of family and laughter and love.

A life Levi couldn't in his wildest dreams have imagined a year ago.

Saying *Yes* to Mount Cowboy was the best play Levi had ever made.

———

For all the latest updates on new projects, sneak peeks, and more, sign up for Layla's Newsletter and join the Layla's Lushes Reader Group on Facebook.

———

Thank you for reading!

ACKNOWLEDGMENTS

Marsh and Levi (and I) promised David (and readers) a wedding, and we finally delivered! A little later than anticipated, but Christmas in July still counts. And would you believe this is actually the first on-page exchange of vows for one of my couples?! Seemed appropriate for the pair who started as a marriage of convenience. I really do love Marsh and Levi so much, and it was a joy to return to San Diego and their merry family, bring in some fun Whiskey Verse cameos, and give everyone the wedding they deserved. And drop some nuggets for future books. Stay tuned!

Thank you, readers, for loving this duo and their family as much as I do and for all your continued support. Thanks as well to the team who helped me bring *Best Play* to life:

Wander Aguiar and Steven Dehler for such an effortlessly sexy photo, and Cate Ashwood for incorporating it into a stunning cover that also features Marsh's beloved bougainvillea.

Kim on beta, Adam Mongaya on edits, Lori Parks on proofing.

Grey's Promotions on publicity.

Christian Leatherman for always narrating Marsh and Levi just right.

And Hailey, Annabeth, Allison, Erin, and my Mermaid GH crew for all the sprints that were critical for getting this book to the wedding on time!

ALSO BY LAYLA REYNE

For the most up-to-date list of titles and a helpful reading order, please visit www.laylareyne.com.

Agents Irish and Whiskey:

Single Malt

Cask Strength

Barrel Proof

Tequila Sunrise

Blended Whiskey

Angel's Share

Fog City:

Prince of Killers

King Slayer

A New Empire

Queen's Ransom

Silent Knight

Perfect Play:

Dead Draw

Bad Bishop

King Hunt

Best Play

ABOUT THE AUTHOR

Layla Reyne is the author of *What We May Be* and the *Agents Irish and Whiskey, Fog City,* and *Perfect Play* series. She writes sexy, intense LGBTQIA+ romance featuring highly competent adults in kitchens, sports arenas, car chases, and other high-stakes situations. Whether it's adrenaline-fueled suspense, rival athletes, vampires and shifters in alt-realms, or love mixed with mouth-watering foodie goodness, queer folks finding happily-ever-afters is guaranteed.

You can find Layla at laylareyne.com, in her reader group on Facebook—Layla's Lushes, and at the following sites:

BB bookbub.com/authors/layla-reyne

f facebook.com/laylareyne

instagram.com/laylareyne

tiktok.com/@laylareyne

www.ingramcontent.com/pod-product-compliance
Lightning Source LLC
Chambersburg PA
CBHW070355310726
48977CB00002B/447